From the Moon, Come in Peace

Paul Nelson

Edited by @DappleGee

Cover Design – Ashley Girres

Inspired by Michael Nelson

"Education is not something you can finish." – Isaac Asimov

*This is a work of fiction. Any character similarities to anyone, living or dead, is purely coincidental.

From the Moon, I Come in Peace.

I am Marcus.

I happen to be autistic.

It's difficult for me to speak because words don't come out in the right order. Writing is better for me. I want to tell you my story. It's really a collection of many stories that go together like a puzzle. These stories have brought me to the place I'm at. I believe everyone must go through good and bad times to grow. I believe we grow most when life is difficult unless the hard times cause us to lose all hope. Sometimes that happens.

Episode One: My Birth

I was born on Halloween night in 1997. My dad often told me about that night. He liked to tell that story. My mother had a difficult pregnancy, so I was born by Caesarian section. As my dad waited for my birth, he heard terrible screaming. He thought it was kids outside being crazy for Halloween, so he didn't think much of it. Later, he found out that a poor woman down the hall, was giving birth to a baby who was thirteen pounds, and the screams were coming from her. It must have hurt very much, but dad said she came through it alright. He got to talk to the parents of the woman, and they said she was very tired but okay. That was a big baby. I don't know why that poor woman did not have a Caesarian Section birth. Anyway, I came into this life to the sound of screams. I think that's kind of funny and perhaps, appropriate.

I didn't cry when I was born. My mom asked, "Is he alright?" The doctor told her I was fine but laughed because I was peeing on his arm as he pulled me out.

Dad said I looked around the room with big eyes at everyone but still did not make a sound. Then, dad looked at everyone and said they began to look concerned. They put me on a table to start cleaning me up. I must not have liked that because I finally began to cry. Then I wouldn't stop crying. Dad said everyone seemed to be relieved after that. He carried me down the hall to the nursery. Now, it was his turn to cry. He cried big tears of joy as he walked down the hall with me in his arms.

For mom, this was the beginning of a bad time. She became sick after my birth. Later, we learned she had lupus and giving birth had triggered it. I always felt sad about that.

I cried constantly after I got to the nursery, so the nurses took me to my mom's room. As soon as I got beside her, I stopped crying. Mom told the nurses to let me stay with her. Dad said that I slept a lot and never cried as long as I was with mom. I guess it made me feel safe to be with her. I think the nurses were glad I was being quiet, so they left me with mom.

We went home. Mom got even more sick. She had a high fever and could not make milk for me, so dad had to take care of both of us. He said I liked drinking formula and slept all night after having my evening bottle. He sang to me as I drank my warm formula. I would stare into his eyes until I started to drift off. It sounds crazy, but I think I can still remember seeing my dad as he stared down at me while I had my night-time bottle. All these years later, that memory is very strong even though I was a tiny infant. After I went to sleep, dad gave mom ice bags for her sore boobies. When we were both asleep, dad carried me to the couch and put me on his chest, where we slept all night. He said it made him feel warm and safe to hold me all night. Eventually, mom got a little better and I started sleeping in my crib. Dad was able to go back to work.

Essay: What is Normal?

For centuries, society has labored to create an image of *normal*. Perhaps this was an unintended development. Perhaps it was an image that was created to bring security to everyday life. Certain behavior was acceptable. One did not deviate from the "norm" without consequences.

White society seems to have a particularly strong sense of *normal*. Much of this stems from what has been perceived to be Christianity. For centuries, and still today, many people who see themselves as good Christians have tiny comfort zones. They latch onto the strict rules and regulations of the Old Testament. To them, that is what Christianity is about. They believe that adhering to rules brings salvation. Yet, some of these people are prejudiced against other faiths, gay people and people with dark skin. They see sex only as a means of reproduction, and completely miss the idea of intimacy, and quite often, love. This strict adherence to rules provides security. However, it also creates stress, abusive behavior and possibly mental health issues. It also pushes the teachings of Jesus into the background. Jesus wasn't all about rules. Jesus came for one reason. He came to show us how to love. This obsession with rules became the backbone for much of America. It became *normal*.

Autistic people do not fit into society's *normal*. There truly is no *normal*. It's understandable that some people may feel uncomfortable around those with mental challenges. Indeed, those who pose a danger should be in a more restrictive environment. However, society must strive to open its doors to autistic people. Learn from them and cherish what they have to teach. Yes, there may be some behavior that could make some feel uneasy. However, when one spends time with an autistic person, the "abnormal" behavior becomes less evident. The person inside is free to emerge. Barriers are broken down. Just as is the case with gay people, those with dark skin, those who speak other languages and those of other faiths, the autistic person is a valuable member of this global society.

Episode Two: Something Is Wrong

When I was two, my dad decided to go back to school for his master's degree, so we moved. We lived in a house close to the university dad attended. After a few months, he was offered a teaching job, so he stopped going to school and worked as a music teacher. Mom was still sick. She seemed to get worse every day. She also worried about me.

"He's not talking," she said. "He just sits and watches television like he's in a trance."

"Maybe he's just slow," dad said. "Some kids don't develop as quickly."

Mom was worried. Nothing dad said calmed her. Everyday mom watched me carefully as I played. I liked my train and truck toys, but I didn't play with them as most kids do. I lined them up, sorted by color. I would lie on my side for hours, staring at my trains and trucks. When I did this, they looked big and realistic, like they did on television. I liked that. Then, I saw an amazing program on television. It was called "Thomas the Tank Engine." I could tell when it was time for Thomas to come on. Dad said I would be doing something in the living room, stop and stand up very straight like I'd realized something important was about to happen. I'd run into the other room and turn the television on just as Thomas was starting. He said it was creepy. I had an internal clock or something. I never missed Thomas. We got Thomas videos, trains, books and sheets for my bed. If I didn't have a certain Thomas engine, I'd take one of my other toy trains and paint it to look like the engine I didn't have. I still love to watch Thomas.

Episode Three: My Diagnosis

When I was three, I was finally diagnosed as autistic. A man came to the house and had me do lots of things and wrote lots of things in a notebook. He finally went over the things he had written down with my parents. He said I was autistic.

My mom took it hard. She started to cry immediately. I think she thought it was her fault. Dad knew, I think. My dad was a big jazz fan. He had a film about Thelonious Monk that he loved. Monk would get up from the piano and spin in circles on stage during a performance. He might have been autistic. I did the same thing, spinning for several minutes while I watched television. I still do. My dad always said this made him suspect that I was autistic. When he found out I was though, it didn't really bother him. He just said, "Well, that's how my boy is."

I started getting helpers right away. People came to the house and played special games with me. As we played, they would write things in a notebook. I guess they were learning about me. The helpers were nice to me and some of the games we played were interesting, so I didn't mind. The games we played helped me prepare for school and reduced my meltdowns.

Essay: What is Autism?

Autism is defined as a developmental disability of the brain. Part of the brain does not develop fully. This causes different problems in different people. Some autistic people cannot speak. Some walk or move in awkward ways because their brain does not control their muscle function properly. Since autism impacts everyone differently, it is referred to as the autism spectrum.

There are many other things that autism may affect; however, one thing that most autistic people seem to have in common is sensory overload. Everything is magnified for autistic people. They are constantly in a state of agitation. Certain noises may be very loud and even painful. Light shining in a window could be blinding to an autistic person. In order to appreciate sensory overload, one might try turning the television to full volume, running the dishwasher, turning the lights on and off quickly while trying to enjoy listening to a favorite song. This creates the intense overload many autistic people feel constantly.

Fortunately, there are measures which help. Some autistic people may wear headphones often. Dark glasses help. Of course, there are many medications which numb the senses.

Routine is vital to those who are on the spectrum because it provides stability. With routine, there are no surprises. Each day is the same. This stable routine is comforting for those who struggle with over-stimulation. Many autistic people use a Velcro picture board. This simple tool gives a visual representation of what will be happening throughout the day, again providing great stability. There are also electronic devices for the same purpose.

Texture is often an issue. Some textures are pleasant while others cause problems. Almost everything is amplified for those who are autistic-noise, texture of objects and food, smells, light.

For me, texture is an issue with food. I like to have my food neat and tidy. Dad cut my food into neat bites, so they were easy to eat. When I eat soup, I don't like the broth. Dad poured most of it out so I could eat "tidy soup." I like the texture of noodles, French fries, most fruits and vegetables, shrimp, rice and chicken nuggets. I cannot tolerate the texture of cereal, eggs, peanut butter, lima beans, coconut, cake and many other baked goods. It's difficult for people to understand that my food desires are often based more on texture than flavor.

I also like to eat certain foods when I'm in certain places. When my grandparents were alive, they took me to their favorite places to eat. When I was with them, they got me a plain cheeseburger with French fries. When my dad took me out, he got me chicken nuggets and fries. At school, I liked to eat from the salad bar. I never ate things in the wrong place. With grandma and grandpa, it was always a plain cheeseburger. With dad, it was chicken nuggets. I didn't mix the two. I never eat *salad at home. That is school food. That is my system of organization and I don't like to change it.*

Similarly, I liked to go to the same places each day with my dad. We would go to the same stores. I didn't want to buy things, I just liked to check and make sure that things were in the same place as the day before. This gave me security. At the bookstore, I wanted to make sure the books I liked were still there and in the correct spot. At the grocery store, I checked on my favorite foods for the same reason. Organization provides stability for me.

Many autistic people have issues with the texture of clothing. Autism parents frequently must remove any labels from clothing. Labels are often a source of meltdowns.

I cannot tolerate long sleeves and ruin any shirt with sleeves past my elbow. I also prefer to be barefoot when inside. After years of trying, dad finally got me to wear socks.

There are millions of other qualities found among those on the spectrum. Many people are puzzled by these so-called quirks. It makes much more sense to simply acknowledge that there are millions of autistic people, and their quirks are really part of who they are. They are unique creations and perfect just as God made them.

Essay: Meltdowns

Meltdowns are a part of autism. Society doesn't really care for meltdowns. It views them as bad behavior. They are not an example of bad behavior or a spoiled child. A meltdown occurs when an autistic person suffers from complete sensory overload. This occurs for many reasons, depending on the individual.

I suffer from overloads when I am in pain, when there is a sound that I cannot tolerate or when I see a bird, bee, or anything that flies. I can stand next to a railroad track when a train passes and not be the least bit bothered. However, when I hear a blender, a hair dryer or an electric weed whacker, I have a complete meltdown.

Most autistic people stim, but this is not necessarily a sign of a meltdown. Stimming can be flapping hands, pacing, making noises or jumping in place. Some autistic people hit their heads with their hands. Many non-autistic people are upset by stimming, but it is how autistic people release tension. Stimming is not always negative. Sometimes, it's a sign of excitement or happiness.

I also hate to poop. I hold my poop, sometimes for days. I'm not sure why I hate it so much.

Maybe it's because of the feeling poop makes inside me. Maybe it's just the mess, but I also meltdown sometimes when I have to poop, and it hurts. My stomach cramps and I begin to get upset. I know I should poop, but I can only poop at home in my own bathroom! I don't want anyone around. That is part of my autism. It's not a behavior problem, it's how my mind is wired. So, if I need to poop but I'm not at home, close to my bathroom, I meltdown.

It's best not to touch or talk to an autistic person when they are having a meltdown. Trying to calm them will only prolong the meltdown. If someone is already melting down, talking or touching will cause further sensory overload. Leave them alone.

Episode Four: My Meltdown Recollections

One of my earliest meltdown recollections is when I was in a big store with my dad. I was little, about three. We were checking out and dad had me sitting in the cart. I was stimming, (flapping my hands). I hit my head on the cart handle and got a big bump. I started crying and couldn't stop. Dad paid quickly and tried to calm me. I got louder. You should never try to calm or restrain an autistic person when they are having a meltdown. Dad hadn't learned this yet. I screamed because it hurt, and I couldn't make it better. My mind was racing with bright colors. Every sound in the store was loud. It was terrifying. No matter what I did, I couldn't calm down. Dad got a cup of ice from a nice lady and put it on the bump but that only made me scream louder. It was cold and that caused more sensory problems.

Then, some horrible woman came up to my dad. She said "If that was my kid, I'd take him in the restroom and teach him a lesson."

Dad tried to explain but the lady had never even heard of autism. She turned to someone standing close by and started to tell him what a spoiled brat I was. People gathered around. Some of them looked upset. Some looked angry. A few offered to help, but they all made more noise, tried to soothe me and patted me. The people who looked angry scared me. My meltdown grew. I cried and screamed for over twenty minutes. When I stopped, I looked at dad. He looked exhausted. He wheeled the cart out to the parking lot, where that same woman was still talking to people about how bad I was. That was the only time I ever saw my dad cry.

The worst meltdown I ever had was at the beach. I was about four years old and had just been diagnosed a few months before. We took a long ride in the car, longer than I had ever been on before. When we arrived, I was tired. We went to the motel first. I began to cry. My routine had been changed. I was in a strange place. I just wanted to lay down in a dark, quiet room. Mom and dad wanted to take me to the beach. They were excited to see how I liked it, but when we got there, the waves breaking on the shore were loud, and the wind was blowing. My sensory overload got worse, and I began to cry louder. Mom thought I might like to put my toes in the water, but it was cold and wet. I began to scream. I thought my head was going to explode and I couldn't tell mom and dad what was wrong. I was so frustrated being trapped in my body, unable to communicate with my senses screaming at me. Mom and dad did not yet understand that less is more. I didn't want to be touched, soothed, have my toes in the sand or be dipped in water. I went into a full meltdown, but dad tried to hold me and comfort me. I screamed and began butting my head. Dad tried to rub my back and soothe me. I head butted him in the nose. Blood went everywhere. He had to let go. I jumped up and down, screaming and flapping my hands for over an hour. Many people who were on the beach tried to help. Finally, dad got the idea. He gave me a beach towel to squeeze and hit on the sand. At last, I worked the stress out and fell down, completely limp, on the sand. Dad sat down, holding his swollen, bloody nose. He learned a valuable lesson that day, and never touched me or soothed me again when I was melting down.

The next morning, I awoke early, feeling much better. We went back to the beach and I played in the sand all day. It was fun. My dad looked tired though.

Episode Five: School

I went to a special pre-school and did well learning my alphabet, numbers and colors. I was well-prepared for kindergarten. I was assigned a wrap-around by the school district since I was autistic and non-verbal. A wrap-around is an assistant. My helper was great. Her name was Nina. She learned a lot about me as she helped me. Nina began to sense when I was getting stressed and needed to go to the timeout area. Sometimes, if I was really stressed, she would take me for a bounce on my therapy ball.

Therapy balls can be used for exercise or working with people who have challenges. My ball came up to about my waist. I learned to sit on it and bounce. It relaxed me. In time, I learned to control it with my butt and thigh muscles. I could keep it underneath me and bounce around the school without even using my hands. Everyone got used to seeing me on it. I even got to bounce around the halls delivering morning announcement papers to all the classrooms. I still bounce on a ball sometimes, but my therapy ball is much bigger now.

I made friends in school even though I couldn't speak. One of my best friends was Mary. Mary didn't care at all that I was autistic. She helped me with schoolwork, played with me at recess and sat with me at lunch. One time, we had indoor recess because the weather was bad. The classroom got very busy and loud. I couldn't take it and had a meltdown. Mary didn't hesitate. She turned off the lights in the classroom, kept everyone back and told them to be quiet. She even got me a soft pillow to squeeze and hit. She was a helper to me, and my best friend. Those were good times, but they didn't last.

My school problems started in the first grade. I still got along with other kids, but we had to do a lot more work. Most of all, we had lots of tests. When we started practicing for the standardized tests we had to take, I couldn't do it. There were lots of questions and lots of tiny round circles that we had to fill in with a pencil. I had trouble reading and it took me a long time to fill in the circles. I wanted to do a good job, but I always felt rushed. I had meltdowns because of the testing. I went home and practiced making round dots on paper.

As first grade progressed, I had more problems. I was stressed most of the time. A few of the kids began to get upset with me. I think they grew tired of my meltdowns and didn't like it that I could leave the room and go bouncing. They wanted to do the same and were jealous. One day, when we lined up to leave the library, I was upset because I didn't get the book I wanted. I started to cry and a boy in front of me told me to be quiet. I pulled his hair. Then we both cried.

Things got worse. I would get so frustrated with the work I couldn't do that I began running around the room screaming. I couldn't explain to anyone why I was so frustrated because I still couldn't say words very well. That made me scream more. I was sick of being trapped in a body that couldn't speak, so I screamed. Finally, a teacher spoke to my dad. He and mom talked. They decided to send me to the special education program.

Essay: Education and Autism

What is the best path for educating an autistic child? This is an agonizing question for parents;

however, the answer is quite simple, there is no set path. Education for any child, autistic or not, depends on the needs and abilities of that child. The education system in the United States is broken. There are too many people trying to run the program-politicians, professors, businesspeople and school board members who never set foot in a school they represent. Education should not be a monetary business. It should be a needs-based industry. Every student's needs must be addressed individually, not as a whole. The idea of assembly-line education is wrong. Every student needs to have an Individual Education Program, not just those with learning disabilities. The people best suited to address student needs are the parents and teachers, working together. Any good teacher can look around his or her classroom and specify the needs of each student.

The question of inclusion for students with learning challenges is a complex one. Inclusion can be wonderful. Many learning challenged students, and adults, want to participate in the same activities as others. There are many wonderful ways to adapt activities so that all may be included; however, inclusion is not always the best path. It is frequently seen as a rule or regulation; that is, everyone needs to be included in the same way. Again, this industrial approach is problematic. Different challenges require different methods of inclusion. If a student is autistic, there may be considerations necessary for avoiding over stimulation, another student may suffer from sensitivity to noise, etc. There are also times when challenged students simply want to work with others who are "like them." Being with others who share challenges can provide comfort and stability. Most people have a group with whom they share common ground. Those with challenges are no different.

One of the greatest problems faced in educating the autistic is the constant attempt by teachers and administrators to make a child "stop" being autistic. Some autistic students are restrained when stimming or experiencing a meltdown. Those who practice this are under the misconception that they can "force" the autism out of the child; however, this practice will only create further problems. There is no need to try to drive autism out of a child. That child is wired that way. It is best to look for ways to help that student adapt.

There are cases of autistic students being sprayed in the face with water every time they stim. The thought is to discourage this necessary reaction to over stimulation or excitement. The proper response is to let an autistic student stim.

It releases tension and anxiety. Teach the other students in the class about why this student needs to do this. It should never be treated as a negative behavior. If the student starts to act aggressively a quiet area should be established in the room, giving that student a safe place to go when feeling overwhelmed. Autistic students should not be restrained. If a student begins to show anxiety, there should be a plan in place for all school personnel who work with that student. This could include time in a sensory room, on a swing, a therapy ball or simply a walk.

The common argument against this is "This takes too much time and is too expensive." Those who make this argument forget that the United States did away with facilities for those with mental challenges. If society is going to include challenged students in schools, there must be provisions. In fact, it is required by state and federal laws. If more emphasis is placed on properly educating and preparing those with mental health challenges for life, many of those would not end up in prison or on the street. Autistic people do not need to apologize for being autistic. Society needs to develop an attitude of acceptance. This is especially true of schools.

Episode Six: Special Education

As soon as I got into special education class, I felt right at home. There were other kids like me in the class. My teacher, Miss Lisa, was patient and took her time teaching us. There was a time-out place where we could go if we needed to de-escalate. I had a therapy ball at my desk instead of a chair. It was comforting to sit on. Gently bouncing on the ball while I worked relaxed my spine. There were only eight of us in the class. I cannot stress how important this was. We all got help when we needed it because the class was so small. It was peaceful and relaxing to be in such a small group. I really enjoyed school again.

However, this was the first time I was bullied. It was the holiday season, and we were working on our holiday performance for parents. The rehearsals went well, but the night of the performance was scary. There were lots of people. It was loud and I was flapping my hands. We were the first group to perform so we were standing in a line at the side of the auditorium. I was nervous. As we waited to go onstage, a man came rushing in. He must have been late because the auditorium lights were going down. He was trying to get to a seat and came barging through our line. He pushed me so hard I fell to the floor. As I fell, I heard him say "Out of my way, retard."

My teacher glared at him, then helped me up. The principal had to wait to start the program because I was stimming so bad. That got the other kids in my class upset and some of them began to stim. My whole class had to go out in the hall for some quiet time. As I stood in the hallway, I wondered what I had done to this man. What could have made him want to say those horrible words and push me down? I didn't even know him. Mom and dad couldn't see what had happened. The teacher told them about it, but also said that we had all worked through it and did well. We did do well too. People clapped loudly for us. I don't like clapping, so I covered my ears, but I was glad people enjoyed our singing.

That night, as we drove home in the dark, I stared out the window of the car, still wondering why that man hated me so much. It hurt.

Most of my years in elementary school went smoothly. I did well in school and made new friends. Occasionally, someone said something I didn't like but not very often. I liked my teachers and my assistant. My memories of that time are happy.

When I went to middle school, things changed. I still had good teachers and the same assistant, but the kids were different. Even some of the kids who had been kind to me in elementary school began to make fun of me. I didn't understand why some of my friends treated me so differently.

One day in the lunchroom, I was stimming. The lunchroom was big and crowded in middle school. It was loud and there was so much going on. I didn't like lunch time because I went into overload. My assistant went back to the classroom to get my headphones that helped block out noise.

As I was flapping my hands, a kid named Dylan walked by and said, "Jesus kid, you look like you're going to take off and fly around the cafeteria." He smacked the back of my head and sat down with his friends. They all laughed. One kid threw a half-full carton of chocolate milk at me.

When my assistant came back, I was having a complete meltdown. My shirt was covered with chocolate milk. I was wet and cold, it was loud, kids were moving all over the room and I was so angry. I began rocking in my chair, then stood up and screamed as I clenched my fists. I hit my hands on the table until they were red. I kept screaming and accidentally knocked my assistant down. Lastly, I threw my lunch across the room.

The Principal came. He was a man who didn't understand autism and he decided to try and restrain me. He stood over me, pushing my shoulders down to try and get me to sit. I head-butted him in the chest and he flew backwards onto a table. He turned red and looked like he might explode, but I think he was embarrassed too so he left me alone. Fortunately, my assistant was able to keep him, and everyone else, back. She put my headphones on me and gave me a dish towel to squeeze and hit against the table. Lunch ended and everyone left except me. I was still calming down. I was exhausted. My assistant was also. We waited until the hallway was quiet and walked slowly back to my classroom.

I learned that my friend Mary went to the Principal's office and reported the kids who bullied me. The bullies had to go back to the cafeteria, clean up the mess and were assigned detention hall. I thought that would be the end of it, but they decided they were going to get back at me.

Episode Seven: Life at Home

About this time, mom got much worse. Her lupus was serious, and it moved into her brain. She stayed in bed all the time. A nurse stayed with her while dad and I were at school. She slept most of the time. Dad was busy when he came home from teaching. He fed me and took a tray of food into mom. Mom and I both had bathroom issues, so that was tough too.

It was hard watching my mom get worse. I began staying away from her room. I would kiss her before school and before bed. She was taking a lot of medications, so her eyes were glassy, and her hair got very thin. It was a little scary. I didn't like to go in and see her like that, but I also loved her and felt guilty if I didn't. Dad looked tired all the time. I know he didn't like seeing her like that either.

Mom had panic attacks often. One day, after school, dad went in the bedroom to give mom her medication. She was breathing very fast, sweating and was having trouble talking. Dad told me she was having a panic attack. A hospice nurse was there. She was very nice. She told me it was alright. Mom was going to feel better in a minute. She gave her some morphine and mom relaxed right away. I don't know what morphine is, but it really seems to relax people. Anyway, mom went to sleep.

Later that night I went in to kiss mom goodnight. She looked much better. I was happy. I kissed her and she told me she loved me. I went to sleep.

The next morning, I looked in mom's room. She was gone. Dad was sitting on the couch. He looked more tired than ever. He smiled, but just a tiny smile. Patting the couch, he said, "Sit here, buddy. I have to talk to you." I sat down. I knew something bad had happened. Dad told me that mom hadn't had a panic attack, it was a heart attack. She had another one during the night and it killed her. He put his arm around me.

"Do you know the last thing mom said?" Dad asked. I shook my head. Dad gave me a squeeze and said softly, "Tell Marcus I love him."

Essay: Life After Death

Many people believe in heaven; however, the perception some people have of life after death is quite odd. They see it as a place where lots of people with wings are floating on clouds, eating chocolates and laughing at cherubs.

What is the purpose of cherubs and where are they from? Are they little kids? Are they servants?

If so, that doesn't seem very nice. Why would heaven make little kids into servants?

Special angels who are pretty, and always seem to be topless, are playing harps for everyone. Everyone in heaven has white skin and there are no dogs or cats.

I don't think this is very realistic since I'm sure dogs and cats go to heaven. Even though little dogs bark and wiggle a lot and I don't like that, I think they go to heaven. Cats are quiet and don't wiggle nearly as much, so I know cats are in heaven. I bet the cherubs like cats, but I think dogs probably scare them.

Usually, Jesus is hanging around somewhere in heaven. He always looks quite pleasant and kind, but if God is shown, He's usually a big man with a white beard, wearing a towel and sitting on a big stone chair. Now, how can a cloud support someone that big on a huge, heavy throne? Also,

God's hair is always flowing around, and He usually looks mad. Maybe He's upset at something the cherubs did, or perhaps He doesn't like harp music. I don't think this is the way life is after death.

My dad talked about life after death sometimes. He thought that what most people call God is a great spirit, much like the Native Americans say it is. This great spirit created the universe, or universes, and everything in it. This spirit is the spirit of love. It created humans to experience the joys and challenges in life. Dad said the pain in life helps us to grow. He said that it hurt to watch mom go through all her pain, but she also brought me into the world, and that was his greatest joy.

Many humans seem to have trouble with love. They seem to want to be like God themselves. They want to be in control and have power over others. That makes them cruel and full of hate. They think they know everything and want everyone to see and do things their way. Dad said that is cultism and it's dangerous. I'm not sure I understand about what a cult is, but I know that many people seem to look down on people who have challenges. They act as if we are less human than they are. That seems to be discrimination and hatred to me, so, I guess that's what dad was talking about with cults.

I think when we die, we go to another level of life. We don't need our bodies anymore, so I guess we are spirits. If we are, I hope we can fly because I would really like that. I could fly around the universe very fast and I bet I wouldn't even sweat. That would be great because I get hot easily and it makes me feel sick. I would fly around and talk to people and see different planets and stars. I would take lots of cats with me. I might take some dogs too, if they were quiet. I'm looking forward to life after death. I think it will be easier for me. I hope people will accept me better in that world.

Episode Eight: Ryan

In middle school, I met my greatest friend. His name was Ryan. Ryan was a lot like me. He was very quiet because his vocal cords did not work. He signed instead of speaking with his mouth. Ryan also used a walker and sometimes had to use an oxygen tank. We sat together in our special education class and in all our other classes too. We liked to read the same kinds of books, we both liked cartoons and movies, loved art class and shared our lunches. Once, we were in a talent show together. That was a great time.

One day, as Ryan and I were taking morning announcements around to classrooms, the kids who bullied me at lunch saw us. They were going outside for gym class. I heard the gym teacher tell the kids to go to the bathroom if they needed to before they went outside. The bullies lied to the teacher and said they were going to the boy's room. The teacher took the other kids outside and the bullies came toward us. I knew we were in trouble. The boy's room was in a secluded part of the school.

The biggest kid spoke first, "So, retards, it must be nice to spend your day walkin' around visiting your retard friends."

Ryan and I turned to walk away. Ryan couldn't go too fast with his walker. The kids knew they had to act fast before their teacher came looking for them. One kid kicked Ryan's walker toward the wall. Ryan went down with a thud, hitting his mouth and chipping a tooth. Another kid held me against the wall while the biggest kid hit me in the stomach. Then they turned to run back outside. As I gasped for air, I heard the big kid say, "Don't say nothin' about this to nobody. Oh wait! I forgot. You're a retard and nobody will believe you." He laughed.

I sat for a long time trying to catch my breath. Ryan had a bloody lip. Finally, a teacher came into the hall. He ran toward us. When he saw Ryan's lip and heard me trying to catch my breath, he asked what had happened. I think he knew. Remembering what the kid said, I told the teacher we were okay. Ryan signed that he was fine too. The teacher said maybe we should go to the nurse. I said we would. I knew we had to do something, or Ryan's mom would call the school to ask how he had chipped his tooth. I took Ryan to the nurse and told her he had fallen. I kept my mouth shut about the bullies. Lots of kids are bullied every day. They know not to talk, or the next beating will be worse.

Essay: Puberty

Puberty is strange. It hit me hard at age thirteen. For me, it came on pretty quickly. I suddenly liked girls and my penis sprang to life. I'm not sure puberty is necessary, but it makes kids do crazy things.

Puberty for autistic kids, and all those with challenges, is just as difficult as it is for everyone-maybe worse. Like everything else for autistic people, it's amplified. Autistic people feel the effects more than others. One of the great problems in the United States is not puberty, it's parents who are afraid to talk to their kids about it.

The United States is a prudish country. It was founded by people who didn't like to talk about sex and that is still true of most Americans.

Parenting is difficult; however, if you are not going to be able to handle the teen years, don't have children. My dad said that a lot.

Parents need to discuss with their kids, including kids with challenges, what happens during puberty. They need to talk about sex, masturbation, abstinence and birth control. Many school health classes do not address these issues. Education is the best weapon in preventing teen pregnancies and sexually transmitted diseases. In addition, condoms should be readily available for teens. Most adults simply treat teens who become parents as bad people. The same is true with teens who get sexually transmitted diseases.

American society too often waits to address problems until it is too late.

My dad had a talk with me about puberty. I began looking at women's legs when we were at the store. I didn't mean to embarrass them, but I really liked women's legs, so I would bend down and stare at them. Their legs were so smooth and soft looking. The first time it happened, dad apologized to the woman and made me do the same. He took me to the side and explained to me that bending over and looking at pretty legs was not polite. He told me it was fine to look, smile and politely say "Hello" to a woman. He said I was never to touch a woman, unless she told me to, but then he said that probably still wasn't a good idea. I did bend over and look a couple more times. I couldn't help it. Dad made me apologize again. Finally, I got good at looking and smiling. I don't say anything, but I still like looking at pretty women's legs. Boobies are fun to look at too.

I was lucky. My dad also talked to me about masturbation. He said it was fine to do in private but not in public. "You don't want to whip it out in the produce department at the store," he said. "You really shouldn't touch yourself down there when you are out in public. Wait until you get home."

"Where can I do it at home?" I asked.

He said that in my bedroom, or the bathroom would be fine.

I am lucky to have had a dad who talked to me about these things. He told me what happens when people have sex, how a baby is born and lots of other things that many kids never learn about. Dad always said that too many don't understand the importance of education.

Essay: When Cuteness Ends

The early years are often easier for kids with disabilities. They are little and cute. This helps people accept them. It's similar to the behavior some people exhibit with pets. When confronted with kittens or puppies, people are mesmerized, but as the animal loses its cuteness, the love affair ends, particularly when effort is required. Dogs need to be walked and cat litter boxes must be cleaned.

The same is true of kids with disabilities. In middle school, their friends from early years begin to migrate toward those who are popular. Some teachers, particularly in the general classroom, grow weary of trying to include disabled kids in their lesson plans. Sometimes administrators simply place challenged students in the most convenient "slot" to make scheduling easy.

Again, this is an example of society turning away and expecting kids with disabilities to fit into the mold and act like everybody else. It will not work. Disabled kids cannot flip a switch and change behavior just because they are older. An autistic child becomes and autistic teen. He or she will not "grow out" of autism.

Episode Nine: High School

By the time I reached high school, I learned to avoid trouble. I stayed with my own gang of friends. We all had challenges, but we watched out for each other. Most of the high school students were pretty kind to us, but there were some who saw us as freaks.

Ryan and I had become such close friends, the teachers suggested we have the same schedule.

We loved having all our classes together. Ryan and I developed great skill with computers, particularly in graphic arts. We also excelled in math, but our favorite subject was lunch. I no longer hated lunch time now that I had a best friend.

One day, Ryan didn't come to school. I managed to put the words together to ask the teacher if he was sick. Mr. Strauss told me that Ryan was having an operation and would be gone for a long time. He explained that this operation was the last in a series that would allow Ryan to walk on his own.

Almost a month later, Ryan came back. The operation worked. He came walking down the hall to our classroom without any assistance. He held one leg to the side, but he moved much faster. All the kids looked at him in wonder. I was so happy to see him that I started flapping my hands and jumping up and down. Best of all, I was asked to take Ryan for walks throughout the day. If he sat too long, he had some pain, so we walked all over the school. He was happy to be rid of his walker, but still had to be careful of his breathing. His lungs had never developed properly, so if he walked too quickly, he started to wheeze.

As I was walking with Ryan, we saw my friend Mary. She was with a big guy. I think he was a football player, so I felt kind of shy. I put my head down and pretended not to see her.

"Hi Marcus," I heard her exclaim. She was genuinely happy to see me, ran over and gave me a huge hug.

"Hello, Mary," I managed to say awkwardly. Talking was still difficult for me.

She visited with me for a long time, holding my hand and giving me lots of hugs, then went back to the boy she was with. Before they walked away, she looked over her shoulder at me and grinned. Ryan looked at me with huge eyes, his mouth wide open in shock.

"She loves you," he signed.

"She does not," I replied. "She's being friendly. That's all." I stumbled as I put the words together. I could feel myself blush and felt really warm inside.

As we walked back to the classroom, I began sniffing the air. I could still smell Mary's perfume lingering on my shirt.

"Oh no," I thought, "I hope nobody notices."

Back in the classroom, Ryan and I sat down quietly. I didn't want to draw any attention to myself, but it was no use. Sheila, the girl next to me, began sniffing the air. She looked right at me and said, "Whoowhee. Marcus smells really sweet. He's got a girlfriend."

Everyone laughed for what seemed like hours. Ryan smiled and put his head down in a book. I turned deep red and sank into my chair.

Essay: Love

Love is difficult for autistic people. As Mr. Spock from Star Trek would say, "Love is illogical."

It seems many people have a difficult time when dealing with love. Love involves letting go and relinquishing control. That is a scary prospect. There is always the chance that one's love will not be returned. Rejection is the result. There are few things people fear more than that.

Falling in love with someone new is quite different from being in love with one's family. Most children love their parents; however, falling in love with a person outside of one's family is an adventure for which few children are prepared. It is awkward for most, and nearly impossible for those who are autistic. What is the best thing to say to someone? Is it proper to touch someone? When is it proper to kiss another?

These issues, and many more, rip at the insides of all young people. Autistic people are no different, but again, the emotions and concerns they feel are tremendously amplified. In addition, they may misinterpret simple kindness and consideration for true love. When the realization comes that they are mistaken and are not actually loved, the result can be devastating, even catastrophic. Love is complicated and confusing

for everyone. It is sheer terror for those with extra
challenges.

Episode Ten: School Dance

Our Senior year, Ryan and I decided to go to the
Senior Prom. We were scared, but everyone else
was going and we didn't want to miss it. We didn't
have dates, so we went together. Ryan wore a
pale blue tuxedo. I wore a dark pin-stripe suit that
my dad loaned me, with a fedora. We looked
pretty sharp.

The lobby of the high school was decorated
with hearts cut out of paper, streamers and lots of
balloons. When we walked in, a photographer
took a picture of each of us. The photographer
had a pretty woman assisting him. She gave us
each a copy of our picture in a cardboard frame.

She told us if we wanted more copies we would have to pay, so we said, "No thank you."

It felt strange walking down the hallway to the gym. Ryan was having a rough night. I think his legs were hurting, so I held his arm. Some people probably thought we were a couple, but I didn't care. So what if we had been? There's nothing wrong with that. Gay people are people just like anybody else. A person's sexual preference is their business and nobody else's.

The music was loud. When we got inside the gym, I put my headphones on. Ryan and I got some punch and stood by the wall. Even with my headphones, the thump of the music was making me stim a little.

There were a lot of pretty girls in tight dresses dancing with their dates. Ryan and I stared at them, then we looked at each other and smiled. We drank some more punch. It was very sweet, but it had kind of a strong taste. I liked it. Ryan did too, so we got some more.

Sheila, from our class, walked over to say hello. She didn't have a date either. She had cerebral palsy. It made it difficult for her to walk and her one arm was badly misshapen.

"You guys look hot," she said.

"Thanks, Sheila," I said. I didn't say anything else. The loud noise was making it hard for me to collect my thoughts so talking was difficult. Sheila put her arm around Ryan. Ryan appeared to be as happy as I'd ever seen him. He had never been to a dance. Until now, he had never been out in public much. Even though the noise was bothering me, I smiled as I looked at my friend. Sheila went to get us more punch. When she got back, the three of us decided to dance together. Some people stared, but most of the couples smiled and looked happy for us. Sheila and Ryan had trouble moving too much so they just bobbed up and down to the music. I began to feel the music and did my best moonwalk. To my surprise, lots of people clapped and cheered. When the song ended, the three of us were laughing and hugging each other. It was a wonderful feeling. I was glad Ryan and I had decided to come to the dance.

The band began the next song. I took another sip of punch and felt very hot. I began to sweat and feel dizzy. I looked at Ryan. He was also sweating, and his eyes were glassy. Sheila was swaying back and forth.

"We need to sit down," I yelled over the music.

"I think we overdid it," Sheila said.

We sat on the bleachers, but the gym began spinning. The other people drinking punch were laughing and acting kind of crazy. Then, a girl on the dancefloor got sick to her stomach and threw up right in front of me.

A chaperone came running over. He looked at us and picked up a glass of punch. After smelling it, he looked at a female chaperone who had come over.

"It's spiked," he said.

"What?" she asked.

"Somebody spiked the punch with alcohol," he explained.

A group of girls helped their sick friend to the restroom. All the other kids just kept dancing and acting crazier by the minute. I began to stim again. I was feeling very uneasy. I realized if the punch was spiked it would be dangerous for Ryan to have more. He was still sitting with Sheila. They were oblivious to what was going on, so I grabbed his cup and stumbled to the men's room. I poured out the punch. My mind raced as the room continued to spin. I went back out to check on Ryan. What I saw was horrible. He had collapsed on the floor. A group of people had gathered around him. One of the chaperones called for an ambulance. Ryan was unconscious and turning blue. I knelt down beside him as someone tried to revive him. He wasn't breathing. A chaperone began CPR.

At last, an ambulance crew arrived and began to work on him. They turned him on his side. He vomited, but he was breathing. They put an oxygen mask on him and started to wheel him away. I went with them. One of the paramedics looked at me and told me I couldn't go in the ambulance. I wanted to speak, but I was so upset the words wouldn't come out. I felt frustrated and helpless. Then, I felt rage. I screamed and clenched my fists. I jumped up and down as my hands flapped wildly. It must have been frightening because when I stopped, everyone stood around the edge of the gym in complete silence.

Exhausted, I walked out of the gym to the main entrance of the school. There was a bench there. I sat down and tried to collect myself. It was almost time for my dad to pick me up. Leaning my head against the wall, I felt a gentle touch on my arm. I turned to see who it was, but my eyes were full of tears. After clearing my eyes, I saw Mary. She took my hand, then put her arm around me. Her head rested on mine. It felt so good to just be held. We sat for several minutes that way. She walked with me to the front door. We waited together for my dad. When he pulled into the parking lot, she gently kissed my cheek and went back to her friends. The next day, I learned Ryan had died.

Episode Eleven: Graduation and Transition

There were only a couple of weeks of school after the Senior Ball. It was difficult getting through the days without Ryan. The police investigated to try and determine who had spiked the punch. Nobody they interviewed would talk. Everyone was scared to say a word since there had been a death. The school put up a plaque in the library with a picture of Ryan, and the Student Council planted a tree in his honor. That was it. My friend was gone, and everyone simply went on their way. I didn't attend graduation. My dad wanted to go, but he knew I was still upset.

Depression overtook my life for some time after that. Not only did I miss my friend, I didn't know what to do now that school was over. Transitioning from school life to adulthood is a tremendous strain for those with challenges. Once again, our routine vanishes. This creates great anxiety. Dad offered some suggestions- a day program, a part-time job or volunteer work. I was too depressed to think about it, so for the time being, dad let me stay home while he worked. I read, watched television and worked on my computer doing some graphic arts.

There were days when I didn't do anything. After dad left, I'd go back to my bedroom, close the shades and lay down. Those days were the worst. I didn't feel sadness or loneliness. I just felt a deep sense of hopelessness. I felt as if nothing mattered, least of all, my life. I spent many days like that - in a dark room with my eyes open.

One morning, after dad went to work, I heard a knock at the door. Usually, I didn't open it. I wasn't comfortable dealing with strangers, but this time, I took a look out the window and saw

Mary standing on the porch. She saw me, smiled and waved.

I opened the door and Mary threw her arms around me. Her blonde hair felt soft against my face. I liked that. She squeezed me and told me how sad she was about Ryan. I didn't say anything.

After she let go of me, she took my hand and led me to the couch.

"Can we sit for a while?" she asked.

I nodded. She put an arm around me and pulled my head against her. I felt kind of uneasy since my face was right above her breast. I knew I wasn't supposed to touch breasts, yet here I was right on top of Mary's. With her other hand, she ran her fingers through my hair. She began talking about how much fun we had in elementary school and how much she missed me when I went to special education. She let go of me and looked right into my face.

"Marcus, you've always been very special to me," she said. "Did you know that?"

My breathing was getting faster. Talking was difficult enough for me under normal circumstances, but now I had a lump in my throat that was almost painful. I tried to say something, but only a gurgle came out. Then, to my utter surprise, Mary gave me a long kiss.

Kissing is strange. I had no idea what to do with my lips or tongue. I tried to return Mary's pucker but I ended up capturing her tongue in my lips. She pulled away a bit and giggled.

"Just relax and press your lips against mine," she stated calmly.

I did what she asked. I tried to relax. It felt nice. Her lips felt so warm. She gently brushed her tongue against mine. I liked that. It tickled a little. I was ready to kiss some more. I held my lips in a pucker again and closed my eyes. There was nothing.

"Oh no," I thought, "I ruined it and she's stopped." I opened my eyes. Mary was standing up removing her blouse. My eyes were wide with wonder and I forgot to stop puckering. Again, Mary giggled. She touched my lips and gently returned them to their usual state. As she removed her bra I gasped. Her breasts were full and beautiful. I had never seen breasts. They are the most wonderful things I know of. I love how soft and round they are. Mary placed one of my hands on her right breast. I squeezed a little too hard.

"Easy," she said with a smile. "Why don't you kiss it?"

I gently kissed her nipple. She groaned a bit and told me that felt good. I placed my hands on both breasts, squeezing gently and kissing her nipples. Now her breathing was getting faster. She pulled away and removed her pants and slid off her shoes. I couldn't believe this was happening, especially in my living room. Sweat was pouring off of me. My heart raced and my penis was so hard it ached. Mary placed a hand on my hard penis and kissed me again.

"Why don't you take some of your clothes off now?" she asked.

I took my shirt off so quickly it ripped. I couldn't get my belt buckle undone because my hands shook so badly. Mary did that for me and lowered my pants.

After that, I can't remember most of the details because I was in a daze. I remember Mary rubbing my penis until I thought it would explode. Then, she stopped and laid me down on my back. After sliding a condom on my member, she got on top of me. Lowering herself down on my throbbing penis, she rode up and down. The feeling was incredible. My mind was alive with flashing colors-vivid and even fluorescent. Watching her breasts as she rode me was more than I could take. I grabbed them and caressed her nipples. She smiled with pleasure.

"Oh yes, Marcus. That's so good!"

I was beginning to understand the word *ecstasy*. Every sound Mary made was intense as a scream, but it wasn't scary. It was joyful and comforting to me. Not only was I having my first sexual experience, I seemed to be doing pretty well. It made me feel wonderful to give Mary such pleasure. I think that must be the difference between *making love* and *having sex*. *Making love* means that you want to bring pleasure to your partner. It involves bonding and feeling generous. *Having sex* means that you are concerned only with your own pleasure. At that moment, I saw Mary as my greatest friend. I remembered all the times she stood up for me. I remembered her holding my hand on the playground, walking me to the nurse when I was sick and sitting with me on the bus. Now, she was giving me one of the most wonderful gifts possible. All I could think of was returning the gift.

Finally, we climaxed together. Mary fell down on top of me. We lay there breathing heavily, but as one, completely in synch. She rested her head on my chest.

"Hey, buddy. That was wonderful," she said.

I smiled. She planted a series of passionate kisses on my lips. This time, I was relaxed and gently returned her warm kisses. She rolled over beside me, and face to face on the big couch, we cuddled for what seemed like hours. With my autistic mind in blissful peace and silence, I dozed off in Mary's arms.

I awoke to Mary speaking softly.

"I have to get going now," she said, brushing her hand against my face.

I gripped her tightly, not wanting the day to end. She put her arms around my neck and smiled as she looked me in the eyes.

"Marcus," she began. "I'm going away. I'm leaving for college in a couple of days. I'm going to school in California. It's a long way away from here. I stopped over today because I don't know when I'll be back. I stopped over to see you because you are so very special to me, and always will be."

A single tear formed in the corner of my eye. Mary gently caught it on her finger. Then, she kissed that finger and placed the tear on my lips.

"No. Don't cry, Marcus. Please don't cry. I wanted us to have this special day. Don't ever forget it. I know I won't."

I nodded. Mary began dressing.

"I want you to make me a promise," she continued. "You must promise me you won't stay inside all the time. You have to get out into the world, Marcus. Will you promise me that?"

"Okay," I whispered timidly. "Sometimes it's scary."

"Yes, it is," she continued, "but the world won't get better without you in it. You need to show people how wonderful and gifted autistic people are. You need to help the world, Marcus. You are full of love and kindness. I saw that from the first day I knew you in kindergarten. Don't let this world make you a prisoner."

She kissed me again and promised to write to me. She knew writing was easier for me than talking on the phone. I got dressed and walked her to the door. We shared one last kiss, then she went down the stairs to her car. Before she got in, she looked over her shoulder, smiled and gave me a sexy wink. I waved as she backed out of the driveway. That was the first and only time I have made love. It remains as the best day of my life.

Essay: Employment

People with challenges are capable of doing many of the jobs available in the workplace. Businesses need to get involved in the programs offered by state and federal governments to include those with challenges in the work environment. To achieve this, the government agencies responsible must improve the benefits for businesses willing to cooperate. Possibly greater tax breaks for businesses would be a possibility.

The benefits of including more people with challenges in the workplace would be tremendous. It would serve to break down many of the barriers that separate society. It would also allow people to experience what autistic people and others are capable of when given the opportunity. Many autistic people, for example, have tremendous computer and artistic abilities.

One must remember it is highly likely that Einstein, Mozart and Tesla were autistic. Consider their achievements. It is terrible to think that others with similar abilities are "locked away" because of their challenges. Everyone has challenges. Not everyone is given opportunity.

Episode Twelve: Looking for Work

I took Mary's words to heart. I would not become a hermit. I screwed up my courage and, with dad's help, looked for employment.

It was determined by the Office of Vocation and Rehabilitation that I was too *high functioning* to qualify for a job coach; however, I received some assistance in finding a job.

I tried working as a custodian at a local factory. The people were kind, but the machinery was loud. I wore my headphones to block some of the noise, but it was still loud, and I could feel the floor shaking from the heavy machines. It was more than I could stand and resulted in a meltdown. It was decided that wasn't an appropriate workplace for me.

I told the man at the Office of Vocation and Rehabilitation that I was skilled with computers. I don't think he believed me. He placed me in a restaurant as a dishwasher. I hated it. The dishwashing machine was loud, and the detergent smelled like chlorine. It made me sick to my stomach. Again, I tried to use my headphones, but the chlorine smell made me throw up.

I took some printouts of my computer graphic work to the man at the Office of Vocation and Rehabilitation. My dad went with me and we both tried to convince him to find me a job working with computers. He looked at the printouts and said," These are very good." Dad and I smiled at each other. It seemed we had convinced him.

My next job placement was cleaning bathrooms and wiping off tables at a fast-food restaurant. The work was boring; however, I got a free burger and fries every day. When the weather was nice, I got to wash the windows. I enjoyed that.

The people who worked at this place were miserable. They were paid so little but had to deal with many mean customers. The employees were nice to me. They appreciated what I did and realized I got paid even less because I was a *special needs* worker.

My friend from school, Sheila, worked there. She worked in the kitchen making burgers. The manager let her sit on a stool due to her cerebral palsy. The work was hard for her, but she tried her best.

The manager was Karen. She liked to hire workers with challenges. She was tall and had a face that looked pretty, but tired. She had a tattoo on her arm that said, "BRIAN, forever in my heart." I thought Brian was an old boyfriend, so I asked her. She explained that Brian was her son.

He died in a car accident. I liked that she had a tattoo to remind her of Brian.

One day, the regional manager came into the restaurant. His name was Ronald, but he made everyone call him Mister Bender. Ronald was a round-shaped man. He had a reddish complexion and spoke loudly. He made us all feel uncomfortable. I always tried to stay away from him. It wasn't that difficult because he usually stayed in the office looking at the computer reports. He would talk to Karen about how sales were down, and she had to do better. Ronald wore shoes that were coming apart, He had placed tape on them but his socks still stuck out in several places.

As usual, he took Karen into the office and closed the door. We could all hear him yelling at her. This was the loudest he had ever been. Everyone got very quiet and worked as quickly as possible. Finally, Karen emerged from the office. She looked pale as she put on her coat.

"Where are you going, Karen?" I asked.

"I've been let go, Marcus," she said, and gave me the best smile she could muster.

"Let go?" I asked. She nodded, turned and walked out.

I looked at Sheila. Both of our eyes were wide, and our mouths open in disbelief. Karen was nice to work for. Why would the Ronald fire her? Sheila began to cry. Karen had trained her, and they were quite close.

Ronald came out of the office, looking most pleased with himself. He was the type of person who needed to feel important, to feel as if he were superior to everyone. Walking up and down the kitchen, he spoke loudly to all us.

"Okay, everyone," he said. "Karen is no longer with the company. She was unproductive. For now, I'm in charge until a new manager is transferred in."

He wasted no time in bossing everyone around, barking commands as if he were a general in the army. People looked scared and started rushing around trying to do things faster. Sheila made the burgers as fast as possible but started dropping lettuce and tomatoes on the floor. The more she hurried, the worse it got. Her bad hand simply could not hold onto things. Ronald came storming over. He picked up the lettuce and tomato slices on the floor and tossed them at Sheila. I couldn't believe it. One tomato slice actually hit her in the face.

"Is this the best you can do, Sheila?" he yelled.

I covered my ears. I didn't want to have a meltdown, or I'd lose my job. Even with my ears covered, his yelling was thundering through my head. I stuck my small fingers deep into my ears to try and block the sound even more. I looked at poor Sheila, now in a complete panic, sobbing and unable to do anything but put her head in her hands. Ronald put his face right in front of hers. I could still hear his words. They were horrifying.

"I don't care if you have a disability. If you can't do this job right, I'll toss your sorry butt out of here and get somebody who can."

I lost control. I saw bright orange and red flashing in my head. I began stimming, jumping up and down and flapping my hands. Then, I screamed, but I didn't have a meltdown. Without thinking, I picked up a mop and ran full speed toward Ronald. In spite of my difficulty speaking, my mouth opened and the following words erupted.

"You bastard!" I cried.

He looked at me in shock. I could tell he wanted to turn and run, but before he could, I hit him square in the belly with the wooden mop handle, knocking the wind out of him. Gasping, he fell to the floor.

"No," he screamed, pulling his knees up toward his chest in self-defense.

Standing over him, I saw terror in his chubby face. He looked like a child who had been caught bullying kids on the playground. The sight of his face angered me more. Again, words of rage poured out of me.

"You're a coward," I said. "You're a coward and a bully."

I took the wet, cleaning end of the mop and shoved it into his face, as if I were brushing his teeth with it. The entire kitchen laughed and cheered as Ronald emitted muffled screams for mercy.

"Karen was a good person," I shouted. You were bad to fire her."

Finally, I stopped. Ronald sat up, grabbed his glasses and spit soap and water out of his mouth. He crawled, like a crab, backwards to the office, stood up, and went in, slamming the door. We all looked at each other for a moment, then could clearly hear the sound of sobbing. That big bully was crying like a baby. A few minutes later, he went out the door, got in his car and drove off. In about an hour, Karen came back. We all cheered and gave her hugs. I never told anybody what happened that day and the entire crew kept silent about it. After work, Sheila gave me a kiss and thanked me.

The next day, Karen called me into the office. I thought I was going to be let go for attacking

Ronald. Karen asked me to sit down. She told me I'd scared Ronald so much that he called the corporate office and told them he made a mistake in firing her. Then, he turned in his resignation.

I wasn't sure what to say. I sat and smiled. Karen put her head in her hands and began shaking. I thought she was crying. Then, I heard her gasp a little-the way you do when you're laughing, and you have to catch your breath. I lowered my head to try and peek at her face. At last, she lifted her head. Her face, red from laughing, wore a huge smile. Tears flowed down her cheeks as she erupted into a deep belly laugh.

"Oh, Marcus," she said. "Thank you so much. You really took care of that bozo. He was such a creep, and I took his crap for two years." We both had a good laugh then Karen gave me a hug.

I worked at the fast-food restaurant for the rest of that year. Eventually, thanks to Karen, I was trained on some of the other jobs, making burgers and milk shakes. I couldn't work the register because some days, I had trouble getting words out. Karen was always patient with me. I will always remember her kindness.

Essay: The Importance of Being Useful

Everyone needs to have a sense of worth. Humans have a need to contribute. For many, this involves employment. Having a job is not only important for financial needs; it is vital for mental health. There are many jobs for which there is no pay and these are of no less importance. In fact, they may be the most important jobs.

There is a woman named Nancy who has come to our house ever since mom died. She sometimes does laundry or bakes something good to eat.

Sometimes, she just sits and visits. I think this is one of the most important jobs; that is, simply being there for others. After mom died, many people stayed away from us. We never had visitors, except for Nancy. Nobody called to ask how we were. Sometimes Nancy and my dad would just sit and have coffee. They would talk and laugh. Nancy understands what it means to be useful.

Episode Thirteen: I Find My Place

Dad came home one day with exciting news. He found a place where they needed someone with my computer skills. It was an advertising business and they liked to hire people with challenges.

"I spoke to them about you, Marcus," he said. "They have a position open and you can go see them tomorrow." He was so excited his face was red. He couldn't stop smiling.

"Okay," I said. "Will you go with me?"

"Of course," he responded. "One of your friends works there. Do you remember Julie from school?"

"Oh yes." I liked Julie. She was very quiet and liked to be with me and Ryan. She was an expert with computers.

The next day, I went to the advertising agency for an interview. Dad went along and introduced me to the man in charge. His name was Mister Platt. I liked him. He was a bald man with glasses and a big mustache that made him look like Teddy Roosevelt. We went into his office to talk. Dad stayed outside.

"I hear you are very good with computers," said Mr. Platt. I nodded and quietly said, "Yes."

Mr. Platt looked at some of my computer designs that I had printed out. He nodded and said, "very good" a lot.

I looked around his office. He had lots of pictures of advertisements framed and hanging on the walls. There was also a picture of a girl playing softball. I got up to look at it. I recognized the girl. Her name was Emily and we had been in school together. She had Downs Syndrome.

"I know her," I exclaimed. "Her name is Emily."

"Yes," Mr. Platt replied. "Emily is my daughter. I told her you were coming in today. She said you're very nice."

Then, we talked about the job. I would be training with Julie. I told him I'd like that. The work sounded interesting. I would be doing artwork for different advertisements. I would start the next day. Julie gave me and dad a tour of the office.

When we got home, dad kept talking about how happy he was that I had a job where I could use my computer skills. He seemed to be as excited as I was. I had trouble sleeping that night but couldn't wait to start the next day.

Episode Fourteen: Working with Julie

My first morning, Julie had a desk prepared for me when I arrived.

"I put your desk by the fish tank," she said. "I thought it would be relaxing for you."

"I like it," I said.

I had an amazing computer with the best graphic arts software possible. Julie began showing me how it worked. I learned quickly and was having a lot of fun. By the end of the morning, she gave me a small advertising project to work on. She asked me if I had any questions.

"I'm okay," I said.

"Great. I'll check on you a little later."

She smiled and patted my shoulder before walking away and leaving me to my work.

I watched her go. Julie was pretty. In fact, I think she was much prettier than when I knew her in school, but I didn't see her a lot then. She had Asperger's syndrome and only had to be in our classroom for English class. She was brilliant in Math and most other subjects, but had trouble writing. Now, I noticed how well-dressed she was. She smelled nice and had long black hair. Her body was curvy, and she moved gracefully. I decided I had better stop watching her and get to work. I needed to concentrate on my job.

I worked for just over an hour on the advertising project. It was an ad for a local coffee company called Martin's. Their slogan was "Martin's Coffee: Rich, Robust and Satisfying." I created a scene of a cowboy sitting by a campfire drinking coffee, while some other cowboys played the guitar and sang. It wasn't that creative, but I thought it looked robust and satisfying. I also added two dogs. One was dancing and the other was taking a drink of coffee out of the pot. When Julie came back over, she liked it so much, she showed it to Mr. Platt. He chuckled and said he liked it too.

"Good work, Marcus," he said. "I'll show that to Mr. Martin. I bet he'll like it too." He was still chuckling as he walked back to his office. Julie smiled at me again and gave me a thumbs up.

Then, she brought three more advertising projects to me. My eyes got big when I saw all the work.

"Welcome to the advertising business," she said. "Why don't you have lunch. You can start on these when you get back."

I nodded.

Episode Fifteen: Sheila

After my first day at work, I felt tired. It was a good tired. I liked my new job and it felt good to use my computer skills. Dad and I had pizza for supper. He wanted to know about my day. As usual, the words came out slowly, but I told him how happy I was with my job. I could tell it made him feel good. He smiled and patted me on the shoulder.

"I'm proud of you, Marcus," he said. "You have a job that you're good at and you enjoy it. Not many people can say that."

I looked over at dad. He looked happy but tired. He started to cough, and his face got red. He had been coughing a lot lately. We both had allergies so I knew that was all it was, but I was worried that he always looked tired.

Dad's phone rang. He didn't want to answer but thought he'd better. He spoke for just a minute and looked upset. He sounded serious.

"I'm so sorry to hear that. Thanks for letting us know," he said as he hung up.

He sat in silence for a moment. Looking at me, a tear formed in his eye.

"What?" I asked.

"That was Nancy," he said. "Marcus, I have some bad news. Your friend, Sheila, died."

"How?" I asked.

"Well, she..." He stopped and looked at the floor. I turned and gazed into dad's face.

"She took her own life. She committed suicide."

Dad put his arm around me, I was limp. Why would Sheila do such a thing? I thought about the day at the fast-food restaurant when I had fought off the regional manager who bullied her. I let go of dad and went to my room, laid down and didn't get up until morning.

Essay: Depression

Depression is not the correct name for this horrible condition. Depression is only one of the many symptoms. Millions of Americans suffer from Depression, yet millions more still see it as a fallacy.

"Get over it and get on with your life" is the common attitude of many.

That attitude is utterly impossible for anyone who suffers from this debilitating condition. For some, depression is more of a chemical imbalance. For others, it can be a complicated combination of mental illness, the result of abuse, physical health problems, chronic illness, the loss of someone close and many other factors.

When depression becomes severe, the result is complete hopelessness. *Hopelessness Syndrome* would be a better name for this disorder. The hopeless stage is when depression becomes dangerous. That is when the loss of purpose can drive some people to take their own lives. Depression is not simply feeling sad. It is deadly.

Episode Sixteen: Recovery

With dad's help, I got back to work the next day. I was so sad about Sheila, but I wanted to work and keep my mind busy. Julie and I talked about Sheila. She gave me a hug and told me to try and be strong.

Somebody new came over to us. I learned his name was Warren. Julie was head of the graphics department. Warren was her assistant. He shook my hand and told me he was glad to have me on board. Warren was tall and very well dressed. He was an African American. He had long shoes. They were the longest I'd ever seen. I wondered if his feet were that long.

Anyway, Warren and I worked together all morning. He had amazing computer skills. He was kind to me. Even though I didn't speak much, he seemed to understand me. We worked hard that morning, right up until lunch time. Julie came over to look at our work and was pleased. We completed three advertising projects. She told us to go to lunch. We were pleased with the work we had done. Smiling, we went to the lunchroom.

My work at the advertising agency brought me great happiness over the next few weeks. I worked happily with Warren every day. We got to be close friends. The enjoyment and satisfaction I found in my work helped with my depression, which gradually vanished. Warren, Julie and I regularly had lunch together. They understood that words came with difficulty for me. They were patient and allowed me the time to get words out.

I liked Julie. She was kind to me, always complimented me on my work, always smiled when we were talking, and gave me pats on the back when I turned in my work. She reminded me of Mary. I began to have strong feelings for her.

One Friday, Warren and Julie asked me if I wanted to go with them on a picnic the next day. I said I did, so we made plans. Julie called my dad that evening to make sure it was okay with him.

"Go ahead," he said. "I plan on doing some napping."

Dad was looking tired most of the time. That worried me. He coughed a lot and had gained weight. He told me it was just a sign that he was getting a little older.

The next day, Warren pulled into the driveway with Julie and another woman. Her name was Kayla. She shook my hand and told me Julie had told her all about me. I sat in the front with Warren. We headed toward the park. It was a warm day. The car windows were open, and we all felt happy.

"I hear you are very good at your job," Kayla said.

I nodded. "Yes, I like it." As I spoke, I turned and looked at Julie and Kayla. They were smiling and holding hands. I turned away quickly.

"Marcus is awesome," Warren said. "We make a great team."

"Yep," Julie added. "I've got the best advertising team at the agency."

I stared at the road, unsure of what was going on between Julie and Kayla. Soon, I realized they were a couple. When we arrived at the park, they held hands as we walked to the picnic area. As Warren started a fire for the hot dogs, I watched as Julie and Kayla exchanged a kiss.

I didn't mind that they were a couple. I was upset because I had fallen in love with Julie. She was always smiling at me and treated me with such kindness. Wasn't that love? Perhaps it was stupid of me to feel hurt, but I did. We ate lunch and took a hike in the woods. It was a beautiful day. The sun was warm. We walked along a stream and saw some deer and a fox, but I could only feel my aching heart.

We hiked for almost two hours then got back in the car. I sat with my head down all the way home. We said our goodbyes. I had already turned toward the house as I heard Warren honk the horn and pull out of the driveway. I went into the house and sat on the couch with dad.

"How was the picnic?" he asked.

"It was good."

I did my best to be cheerful. Dad made popcorn and we watched a movie. I thought of how glad I was to have dad in my life. He was always there, never seemed to want anything for himself and was always happy to be with me. I knew who he was and always would be. He was my rock.

Essay: Autism and Perception

It is difficult for many autistic people to understand subtle things. Noticing facial expressions, nuances, and understanding humor can be almost impossible. The autistic mind is frequently a literal mind. Much like a binary computer, the autistic brain is a computer that analyzes things in a series of zeroes and ones, black and white, yes and no. Perhaps the part of the brain that is not as developed in autistic people is also responsible for the perception of subtle details.

However, many autistic people are also blessed with remarkable abilities. Some have tremendous ability in math and can instantly do complex calculations in their heads. Many are able to play the piano masterfully at age three or four with no training, or to draw perfect scenes from memory with paper and pencil. Many brilliant people have been autistic and have made great advancements in society. Some pioneers who were probably autistic include Tesla, Einstein and perhaps Mozart.

One must wonder if these abilities are locked in everyone's brain but need some sort of "switch" to be flipped in order to release them. What if autism is that switch? For centuries, autistic people were placed in institutions, usually by age thirteen. How many Einsteins were simply locked away and forgotten? How many symphonies worthy of Mozart could another person have composed? Again, the prevailing reason was society's inability to accept the mysterious, the unique and the unknown.

Episode Seventeen: Focusing on Work

I concentrated on my work after the picnic. I was determined to avoid relationships. Even close friendships had been too painful. Warren and I worked well together, but I begged off anymore invitations to social activities.

My determination paid off. I was awarded the "Employee of the Month" award for the next four months. Advertisers began to ask for me to create ad campaigns. It was an honor, but most of all, I was enjoying my work. That was greatly satisfying for me, and I was most pleased to see my dad feeling so proud. He hadn't shown much joy since mom had died. He had simply been too busy and overwhelmed to enjoy life. I smiled as I took each award home. Dad was so proud, he had tears welling up in his eyes. It was a happy time.

Episode Eighteen: A Tragic Day

Saturday mornings were special for dad and I. We started our weekend with a big pancake breakfast, then took a long walk together when the weather permitted.

One Saturday, we were busy preparing breakfast. Dad asked me to take some garbage out to the trash can. I bagged it and went outside. The weather was sunny and warm. As I walked back, I smiled and thought how nice our walk would be after breakfast.

I walked into the house and found dad on the floor. He was having trouble breathing and said his chest hurt.

"Marcus," he said, "Get me an aspirin." I did and he put it under his tongue. He was sweating and breathing very fast.

"Now," he continued, "get my phone." I handed him his phone. I felt scared and my palms were sweaty. I knew something serious was wrong. I wanted to help but didn't know what to do. Dad was doing his best to remain calm. He dialed 911. He told the person on the phone he was having a heart attack. My heart raced when I heard that.

"A heart attack," I thought. "No. This can't be happening. I need dad. He can't die."

Dad gave the dispatcher our address. He looked at me and attempted a smile as he put his head down on the floor.

"It'll be okay," he said. "The ambulance will be here soon. I need to go to the hospital, but you can come too. It'll be okay, Marcus."

I sat down beside him and patted his head.

"It's okay. It's okay," I said, remembering how many times he had said that to me.

I began rocking back and forth nervously. I was determined not to have a meltdown. Dad needed me to be strong. I held dad's hand the way he held mine when I was sick. He smiled and told me that felt good. I rocked back and forth. I couldn't help it.

The paramedics got to our house right away. They started putting tubes and needles in dad and placed an oxygen mask on him. That seemed to help. I smiled. One paramedic was a woman and the other a man. The woman had red hair. It reminded me of mom's hair. The man had dark skin and was very strong. He looked like he could have picked dad up if he wanted to.

"It's okay," I said. "Dad's okay."

"He's stable," I heard the woman say.

They wheeled dad to the ambulance. I got in the back with the woman paramedic and dad. I knew it was serious because they turned on the siren. When they use a siren in television shows, it's because something bad is happening. That made me feel nervous again. It was so loud. I covered my ears, still rocking, as the ambulance sped to the hospital. I had never gone that fast in a car before.

At the hospital, I had to sit in a chair by the table where doctors and nurses worked on my dad. I could occasionally see dad's face. He was very pale and sweat poured off him. I began to do vocal stimming. Dad wasn't getting better. He was getting worse. He tried to speak, but it was difficult because he was gasping.

"That's my son," he said. "He's autistic. He needs me."

"Calm down," a nurse said, trying to sound soothing. "You have to relax."

"No," dad gasped. "You don't understand. Nobody can take care of him like I can. Please! He needs me. I know how to cut his food the right way. You have to cut it in bites for him."

"Please, calm down," the doctor said.

"My son needs me," dad cried. "I can't die. Nobody knows what to do." Dad tried to sit up. "I have to give him his medicine. It's time for his medicine. You don't understand. Nobody else can do it right. One of the dosages was changed and I'm the only one who..."

A nurse pushed the mask back down over dad's nose and mouth.

"You have to lay down," a doctor exclaimed as he pushed dad back down onto the table.

There came a horrible sound from dad's chest. It sounded like a gurgle and a rattle at the same time. Dad fell back onto the table. He wasn't moving. The doctor started pounding on dad's chest. A machine on the wall gave out a long beep. Then, everyone began working very fast. I knew it was bad. They used some electric paddles to try and make dad's heart start again. Dad's body leapt up off the table. The machine kept beeping, so I knew he wasn't breathing. I grabbed my head and rocked faster. They used the paddles two more times. There was still beeping. They stopped working. The room grew silent. Everyone looked down at the floor. Nobody moved until a nurse walked slowly over and sat beside me. She took my hand in hers, as I rocked. I started crying. Dad was dead.

Essay: The Autism Parent's Nightmare

Autism parents, particularly single parents, have a common nightmare; however, it is not only present when they sleep. It lives within them twenty-four hours a day and lasts until the end of their lives. That nightmare is:

"What will happen to my child if I die?"

A parent may make plans for the care of his or her child. In most cases, the plans will be carried out. However, if a parent dies unexpectedly, problems may arise. Parents may intend for their child to become a resident in a group home but waiting lists for group homes are long. It might take years for there to be an opening. In some cases, disabled children have been placed in the first available slot, perhaps hundreds of miles away. This can be traumatic and even disastrous. A friend or family member might intervene, sometimes with dishonest intentions, such as obtaining access to the child's financial assistance. The possibilities can be seemingly endless and add greatly to the nightmare. Parents of autistic kids learn to live in mental exhaustion.

Episode Nineteen: What to do?

After dad died, my depression was unbearable. I simply stayed in bed in the dark. Nancy spent most of the day looking after me. She cooked, cleaned and washed my clothes, but had to leave by late afternoon to care for her mother.

I began to think the world was simply not a place for me, and started thinking of ways to take my life. Perhaps I could take an overdose of my medications; however, I wasn't sure if psychological drugs would kill me. Sheila hung herself. I wasn't sure I liked the thought of strangling. I wasn't good at tying knots either, so the whole thing might come loose, and I'd simply fall to the floor. I considered a gun but didn't know where I could get one. I also didn't have access to money. Dad had taken care of my finances. I kept the thought of suicide in my mind, but mostly just stayed in bed, feeling nothing but hopelessness.

Eventually, there was a hearing I was required to attend. It was to determine where to place me. I sat silently in the judge's chambers, feeling hopeless, alone and frightened. Nancy was by my side but I wasn't aware of anything but the darkness surrounding me.

I did hear bits and pieces of a conversation between the judge and my case manager. I remember hearing them discuss whether I could live alone. The judge argued that since I was employed, this might be possible; however, my case manager stated that I had severe communication limitations in the event of an emergency, and that I could not safely operate a stove or other home appliances. I frequently forgot to wear a coat when it was cold. The judge finally dismissed that idea.

Next, they considered group homes, which were all full. The case manager inquired about an apartment where I could have a roommate and a live-in companion to care for me. Again, there were no openings. Finally, there was the mention of moving me to a facility in a large city, hundreds of miles away. At this point, I felt fear welling up inside. It felt like I might vomit. With horror in my eyes, I looked at Nancy. She patted my hand, abruptly stood and interrupted the discussion.

"I would be happy to temporarily move in with Marcus," she exclaimed.

The three of us looked at Nancy in surprise. For the first time in weeks, the corners of my mouth turned upwards in a tiny smile.

"Are you sure, Miss Hamlin?" the judge queried.

"Yes, until a permanent arrangement becomes available, an arrangement Marcus is comfortable with," she replied. She sat back down and held my hand.

The judge and case manager spoke quietly for some time. Nancy put an arm around me.

"It's okay. We'll get this settled Marcus," she said calmly. I laid my head on her shoulder. The judge saw this. He smiled before he spoke.

"If you are comfortable with this Miss Hamlin, I feel this is the best arrangement for Marcus at this time. The court thanks you for your dedication. Marcus, I'm truly sorry about your father and I wish you the best of luck. We will convene again in six months to evaluate the situation and to see if any other options have become available. Is that acceptable to you, Marcus?"

I nodded. "Yes."

Essay: Facilities for Those in Need

There is a crisis in the world. There are few facilities to care for those in need, particularly those with mental illnesses and mental disabilities. Perhaps it is worse in the United States than anywhere else. Worse, because the United States is a country that prides itself on being wealthy and prosperous, yet there are so many who cry out for help. That cry is met most often with silence and even condemnation.

If someone is physically ill, the common response is sympathy. Many people devote a great amount of time and money to fighting physical illnesses, such as cancer, heart disease, diabetes, etc. Many people devote the same type of energy and money to helping animals. Those are certainly worthy causes. However, mental illnesses and mental disabilities are given a blind eye by many, except for families who have felt their impact firsthand. The common response to those who suffer from these mental challenges is often one of shame. Perhaps it is due to the large number of people with mental challenges who suffer from addiction.

"He's just a lazy druggie. He can't do anything right," are common remarks.

While there are certainly people for whom this may be true, there are many cases where these attitudes are aimed at those with mental challenges. The reason for high addiction rates among the mentally challenged is frequently a lack of help provided by society. Frequently, people with mental health issues have no one to care for them once they reach a certain age. If they require medication to modify behavior, there is nobody to monitor their medication and see that it is given properly.

In school, many students with severe mental needs are simply passed down the line. Society treats mental issues as behavior issues. Rather than treating the source of the problem, society puts a "band aid" on the matter and waits until someone with mental issues becomes a threat to the safety of others.

Although they were not the perfect solution, the United States did at one time have Federally and State-funded mental facilities. Some were horrible, but others did their best at providing a safe environment for residents. Many even grew crops to sell and provided other basic employment for residents. Americans decided they didn't want their taxes to pay for such facilities. This is one of the greatest reasons for the increase in homelessness in the United States. Many people with mental challenges have nowhere to go.

Episode Twenty: Enlightenment

After the hearing, I was still unsure of what to do with my life. Depression still ruled my life. I missed dad terribly. Nancy was a great comfort, but I still had a terrible emptiness inside. I hadn't worked in weeks.

One morning, after Nancy was at the store, I sat at the kitchen table drinking coffee. I was feeling hopeless again. My thoughts were dark and frightening. As I took a sip of coffee, I felt warmth growing inside me. I thought it was simply the coffee at first; however, it continued to grow. I began to feel alarmed. Was I ill? What was wrong? Then, I smelled it. I was surrounded by the smell of the most incredibly sweet perfume imaginable. I looked around to see if Nancy had come back to the house. She had not. I was alone. The warmth continued to swell within me as If I were receiving a loving hug. The smell of perfume filled my nose and then my lungs. I suddenly felt completely at peace.

Closing my eyes, I felt a presence. It was my mother. I know it. She was there in the kitchen with me. She wanted me to know that I would be okay. I heard her say, ever so clearly,

"Marcus, you have to live. You cannot hide away. You matter."

As quickly as it had appeared, the sweet smell vanished.

I sat for a moment in wonderful bliss. I could still feel the warmth. My depression had disappeared. For the first time, I felt like showering, shaving and getting dressed. When Nancy arrived an hour later, she was stunned to see me looking so well. I was listening to music.

"Nancy, I want to work tomorrow," I said. The words flew out of me with no difficulty.

She smiled and promised she would drive me to work the next morning.

Essay: Never Stop Learning

It seems that many people feel they know everything by the time they are adults. This is a mistake and perhaps the source of many problems in society. Ego is a powerful opponent for most people. There is a strong desire in many humans to be gods. This is tragic. Learning and growing are essential to happiness. When someone feels they have learned all that is necessary, the result is often anger and bitterness toward everything that doesn't fit into that person's ideal world. That can result in bigotry and hatred.

I like to call these people "tiny brains." Those with a big ego seem to have tiny minds that are completely closed.

One must strive to keep the mind open to new ideas and learn right up until the last moment of life. This could be what Christ spoke of when He said, "To enter the Kingdom of Heaven, one must have the mind of a child." It is essential to keep the mind innocent and open to new ideas.

Episode Twenty-One: Deciding on My Path

With Nancy's help, I eventually began riding the bus to work. I didn't want to be a bother by asking her to take me to work every day, and I wanted to show that I could be independent. Warren and

Julie were happy to have me back. I immersed myself in work and found keeping busy greatly helped my depression. Work was also important for another reason. I knew dad was proud of me and didn't want to let him down.

Julie and Kayla regularly had pizza nights and Warren and I always attended. It didn't matter to them that speaking was difficult for me. The more time we spent together, the more they seemed to know what was going through my mind. We began to communicate through gestures, smiles and hugs. I found a new family.

Eventually, I moved into a group home. It was hard to say goodbye to Nancy, but we still get together sometimes for lunch. Her mother died so she has more time now. Nancy has tired eyes that have seen many difficult times, but she is still kind.

I like the group home. My roommate is Pete. He is autistic and loves drawing. He draws beautiful scenes with animals. He also has trouble speaking, but we understand one another. Two other men live in our group home. Their names are Walt and Mike. Walt has Down's Syndrome. He loves to cook and is very good at it. He makes the best Italian food I've ever had. In fact, since I've been at the group home, I've gained eight pounds.

Mike is an older gentleman. I don't know if anyone knows what his condition is. He's pleasant but very quiet. He can talk, but frequently chooses not to. He lived on the street for years. Mike loves to read and do crossword puzzles-the really hard ones.

We also have a cat named Edward. He is gray and likes to sleep on my head all night.

The group home gives me the safety and security I need. We have a routine. Every night, we watch television. Mike usually decides what to watch. We make popcorn just like dad and I did. It's a good place to call my home.

Kayla and Julie are married now, but Warren and I still spend lots of time with them. Tomorrow, they are picking me up. We're going for a hike in the woods. Then, we will go out for pizza. I get to pick the toppings.

I still have days where I battle depression. I take medicine that helps. It's still hard to watch the reaction some people have to those with mental challenges, and it hurts to think about some of the things that happened in my life, but it helps a lot to have so many people who care about me. That's what matters most. That's what everybody wants.

I hope for a day when autistic people will be seen for what they are; not for what they are not.

The End

Made in the USA
Monee, IL
04 April 2021